W9-CDP-345

RUNAWAY HIT

Adapted by Lara Bergen

Based on the series created by Dan Povenmire & Jeff "Swampy" Marsh

DISNEP PRESS

New York

Copyright © 2009 Disney Enterprises, Inc.

All rights reserved. Published by Disney Press, an imprint of Disney Book Group. No part of this book may be reproduced or transmitted in any form or by any means, electronic or mechanical, including photocopying, recording, or by any information storage and retrieval system, without written permission from the publisher. For information address Disney Press, 114 Fifth Avenue, New York, New York 10011-5690.

Printed in the United States of America
1 3 5 7 9 10 8 6 4 2

Library of Congress Catalog Card Number on file.
ISBN 978-1-4231-1797-1

For more Disney Press fun, visit www.disneybooks.com.
Visit DisneyChannel.com

If you purchased this book without a cover, you should be aware that this book is stolen property. It was reported as "unsold and destroyed" to the publisher, and neither the author nor the publisher has received any payment for this "stripped" book.

Part One

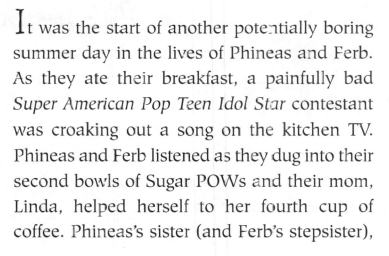

It was the start of another potentially boring summer day in the lives of Phineas and Ferb. As they ate their breakfast, a painfully bad *Super American Pop Teen Idol Star* contestant was croaking out a song on the kitchen TV. Phineas and Ferb listened as they dug into their second bowls of Sugar POWs and their mom, Linda, helped herself to her fourth cup of coffee. Phineas's sister (and Ferb's stepsister),

Candace, was searching in the refrigerator.

"*I . . . met my love in a—*" the boy on the show belted out at the top of his lungs, sounding a lot like a human bagpipe, only worse.

As the boys watched, a big boxing glove shot out of nowhere and—*BOOM!*—whacked the contestant off the stage.

"Oh, boy!" cried the announcer. "Did that kid stink or what? Ha!" He laughed and 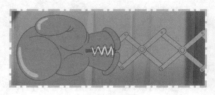 shook his head, then grinned and pointed at the camera. "But maybe *you've* got what it takes to be . . ." as he spoke, the words flashed onto the screen: ". . . the next . . . *Super . . . American . . . Pop . . . Teen . . . Idol . . . Star*!! Auditions open today at the Googolplex Mall in beautiful downtown Danville!"

Candace immediately gave up her search

for a raspberry yogurt and ran to the television. "Auditions! Today!" Her heart was pounding in her chest. Was it possible? Was her favorite show really having auditions at the local mall?

"Yes!" said the announcer cheerfully. "Today! At two o'clock sharp!"

"*Yes!*" Candace lifted the TV off the counter and planted a big wet kiss in the middle of the screen. "*Mwaahh! I've got to tell Stacy!*" She dashed off to her room to call her best friend right away. After all, opportunities like this didn't just up and land in a girl's very own hometown every day!

Unfortunately, Candace forgot that she was still holding the television set. And it was still plugged into the wall. . . .

"Oh!" she cried, as her arms flew back and —*THONK!*—her rear end hit the floor.

Phineas and Ferb glanced at Candace from their seats at the kitchen table to see what all the noise was about. Then they went back to eating their cereal.

"That pop-star stuff might be fun at first," said Phineas between spoonfuls. "But then you'd be stuck in a dead-end job. Too bad you can't just do it once and move on."

"Well, what you're talking about," said Linda, taking another sip of coffee, "is a one-hit wonder." She walked over to the counter and stood next to the TV.

"A one-hit wonder?" said Phineas, looking up. "What's that?"

"Well . . ." Linda began. She put her finger to her chin as her eyes drifted dreamily to the ceiling. ". . . A musical act goes to the top of the charts with a catchy tune and meaningless lyrics."

Then her smile was quickly replaced with a frown. "Then they throw a big diva tantrum," Linda went on grimly, "lose their label, and fade to obscurity. Before you know it, their song ends up as elevator music. Years later, they have a reunion concert . . ." She sighed and seemed to drift further away. "And after that they never sing again . . . and no one remembers them."

Linda's eyes snapped back into focus. She smiled and touched her chest. "Ha! Not that *I* would know anything about that!"

Then, humming a little song, she walked out of the room.

If you say so, thought Phineas, exchanging a baffled look with Ferb. For a mom, she sure seemed to know a lot about it.

7

Phineas shrugged. As Linda was giving her description, he'd made a list of all the things needed in order to be a one-hit wonder. Now he read back over what he'd written down.

"A one-hit wonder . . ." he said.

"Ferb!" he said excitedly. "I know what we're gonna do today!"

But Ferb was always a beat ahead of his stepbrother. He'd already strapped on an electric guitar and was ready to go!

Chapter 2

Later that morning, in Candace's room, Stacy watched calmly as her best friend freaked out. This was the opportunity Candace had been waiting for her whole life! What better way to get out from under her unbearable brothers' unbearable shadow once and for all? There was no question that she had as much talent as any other Super American Pop Teen Idol Star . . . if she did say so herself. Singing and

9

acting were *her* thing. (Not Phineas and Ferb's!) Now she finally had a way to get all the fame and fortune she so totally deserved.

But first she had to ace the auditions.

"Stacy," Candace wailed as she thumbed through her CDs for the umpteenth time, "what am I going to *sing*?"

"Hel-*lo*?" said Stacy, whose mind was, as usual, on the most important matters at hand. "What are you going to *wear*?"

Hmm, thought Candace. Good question.

Quickly, she moved to her closet.

"What do you think?" she asked, slipping into a long blue gown.

"Too much," Stacy replied.

So Candace tried on a bathing suit.

"Too little," Stacy said.

She tried on a pinafore.

"Ugh." Stacy groaned. That was way too clean.

She changed into torn cords and a hippie T-shirt.

"Too dirty," Stacy said, scrunching up her nose.

Stacy sat up and eagerly examined Candace's next outfit. It was an '80s pop-star getup, complete with white boots, pink leg warmers, miniskirt, and acid-washed jacket. "Hey!" she said, pointing. "Where'd you get *that*?"

"In my mom's closet. You like it?" Candace asked, turning from side to side.

Stacy reconsidered. "Nah," she said, "Too retro."

So Candace kept on trying—throwing on everything from a police uniform to a gorilla suit—until at last Stacy stopped her with a decisive *"Perfect!"*

"Nice, huh?" said Candace, smiling. She was wearing the exact same red top and white skirt she wore almost every day.

"Yeah," said Stacy. "You should have tried that on first."

Eagerly, Candace handed Stacy her purse. "Let's go!" she cried.

Candace was so focused on getting to the mall in time for the *Super American Pop Teen Idol Star* auditions, she didn't even notice Phineas and Ferb in their room as she ran past.

The boys were both hard at work. Ferb was at the computer, and Phineas was on the floor with a pencil and a notebook. A rhyming dictionary was close by.

Phineas nodded his

head. "Meaningless lyrics done!" he exclaimed. Then he looked at Ferb. "How's the catchy tune coming along?"

Ferb hit a key, and a solid A-flat sounded.

"Excellent!" said Phineas. "We'll be done by lunch!"

Then he looked around the room. "Hey, where'd Perry go?" The mild-mannered platypus, Phineas's reliable pet, had been lounging by Ferb's bed just a moment earlier. . . .

Little did Phineas, Ferb, or anyone else in their family know that their pet, Perry, wasn't just any old platypus. Oh, no. When he wasn't lying around and making weird chirping noises in front of the boys, he was off

13

defending the world from his archnemesis, Dr. Heinz Doofenshmirtz, evil genius (to use the term loosely) extraordinaire.

And that's exactly where he was headed that day.

Out in the hall, with a quick glance over his shoulder to make sure nobody was watching, Perry popped up on two legs and ducked into the nearest bathroom.

The door closed—*SLAM!*—and with a flush, Perry was gone. He was whisked down through the plumbing to his secret hideout under Phineas and Ferb's house.

Unlike Phineas and Ferb's modest suburban home, Perry's headquarters were outfitted in high-tech equipment and surveillance devices. There were jet packs and space suits and a closet full of clever disguises, plus an entire wall of high-speed computers and satellite feeds.

"Hello . . . hello? Anybody there?" A giant, white-mustached face stared out from an enormous high-def screen at the center of Agent P's cave. It was Perry's superior officer and  mission-assigner, Major Monogram, looking lonely and a little confused.

"Oh!" he said, relieved, as Perry landed with a *SPLASH!* in front of him. "Good morning, Agent P! We've just received word that Dr. Doofenshmirtz has been buying up construction toys at an alarming rate. We need you to find out what he's up to and . . . put a stop to it!"

Perry raised his front paw in an "aye-aye" salute and was on it in a flash.

 15

He hurried over to his fleet of spy vehicles—he had everything from a jet-powered skateboard to a nuclear submarine—and chose a sleek-looking motor scooter. He leaped on and gunned the engine as a hydraulic lift in the floor began to raise him to the street. When he reached the surface, the road flipped to let him through. And with a deep *BRRUMMM!* he was off.

Of course, even supersecret agents on urgent missions have to stop at red lights. (It's the law, after all.) The last thing he expected,

however, was for Phineas and Ferb's mom to pull up right beside him on her way to the mall with Candace and Stacy. He turned and—*gulp!*—saw Linda turn his way.

Good thing he had a fake mustache, nose, and glasses handy! Perry slipped them on and disguised himself just as Linda did a double take, mouth agape and eyes wide.

Huh? thought Linda, taking a closer look at the scooter rider alongside her car. He looked oddly familiar. Could it possibly be . . .

But the next thing Linda knew, the light had turned green and the mysterious character was gone.

Chapter 3

Later, at the Googolplex Mall, Candace and Stacy were ready to win!

"We'll meet back at the entrance in an hour," Linda told them.

"Come on, Stacy," Candace urged her friend, practically dragging her past the key-chain booths and sunglasses stalls. "We gotta hurry so we can get a spot in li—"

Candace's jaw dropped to the floor as they

stepped up to join a
line that seemed to
go on and on for
miles. Her eyes fol-
lowed the line as it
wound its way to the
spotlighted stage.

All of a sudden she felt . . . *nervous!*
Nervous was not something Candace was
used to feeling. "I've never sung in front of so
many people!" she gasped.

Stacy tapped her on the shoulder. "Uh . . .
Candace?" She motioned over her shoulder to
the even larger crowd of spectators standing
on the other side.

"Ugh!" Candace's nervousness quickly
turned to panic. "I can't do this!" she squealed.

"Oh, yes, you can!" said Stacy. She took
Candace by the shoulders and looked her in
the eye. "You're not a quitter, you're a fighter!"

"I am?" said Candace meekly.

"Sure you are," said Stacy. "You're a lean, mean, singing machine."

The pep talk worked. Candace squared her jaw and made fists with both hands. Then she attacked Stacy's purse as if it were a punching bag and she were the heavyweight champion of the world.

"*Grrrr!*" she growled, working herself into a frenzy.

"That's it!" Stacy encouraged her. "Yeah! Now you're looking like a winner."

Candace threw one more round of punches. Then she doubled over, exhausted. She was dripping with sweat, her hair was a mess, and she was panting like a dog that hadn't had a drink for days.

"Hey, Candace."

She froze. No! It couldn't be . . . she thought.

She looked over her shoulder. Yikes! It was!

Jeremy. The object of her biggest, most ginormous, crush ever!

She hurriedly smoothed her hair and tucked her blouse back into her skirt.

"And *that* is what a gorilla looks like when you try to take away his food," she said brightly to Stacy. She laughed and turned around. "Oh! Hi, Jeremy!" She  hoped she looked convincingly casual and surprised. "Are you auditioning, too?"

"Nah." He held up the small white music player he was holding in his hand. "I came to see this hot new band called P.F.T. I downloaded their song this morning. It's *tight*! The hundredth contestant gets to sing onstage with the band!"

"Really?" said Candace. She checked the

line to see how close she was to getting to the auditions. She and Stacy had moved pretty far along; there were just a few more people between her and the entrance turnstile. She sighed and kept smiling back at Jeremy as she followed the line in front of her. Funny that she'd never heard of this awesome new band before, she thought, as she finally passed through the contestant turnstile.

Ding-ding-ding-ding-ding!

All of sudden, a bell had started ringing, and a giant sign reading 100TH CONTESTANT began to flash on and off.

"Hey," said Jeremy, "looks like that's you!"

And sure enough, up stepped the *Super American Pop Teen Idol Star* announcer to grab Candace by the arm and whisk her away.

"Congratulations!" the announcer declared as he pulled her toward the stage. "You're the one-hundredth contestant!"

The next thing Candace knew, she was

standing in front of a microphone, facing an enormous crowd. She couldn't believe it—she was about to live her dream!

"Ladies and gentlemen . . ." the announcer's voice boomed, ". . . this young lady has the honor of singing onstage with P.F.T. So now . . . the band you've been waiting for . . . Phineas and the Ferb-Tones!"

At first, Candace was thrilled. But a moment later her mouth dropped open as the eager crowd erupted into screams and she realized what the announcer had said. She turned, and, sure enough, Phineas and Ferb emerged

23

like rock stars from a thick, dramatic fog. This was no dream, she quickly realized. This was a nightmare!

"Phineas?!" she cried.

"Candace?" Phineas walked toward her across the stage, carrying an electric guitar. "You're the hundredth contestant? How *serendipitous!*" He grinned and pointed back and forth between the two of them. "This'll be like a brother-sister thing! Now," he went on, pulling a sheet of music out of his pocket, "I'm assuming you've heard our single. I mean, who hasn't? Right?" He shrugged. "It's a big hit." He handed her the paper. "So here are the words, but don't worry if you get lost. The lyrics are meaningless anyway." He winked as he strode back across the stage toward Ferb. "I'll point when it's your turn."

Candace watched him, speechless, as he took his place next to Ferb, who stood ready at a keyboard. Beside them, like backup singers, smoothly swaying to the beat, stood their friend Isabella and three of her fellow Fireside Girls. Isabella was never far from the members of her scout group.

"Ladies and gentlemen," said Phineas, gesturing to Isabella and the girls, "the Ferbettes!"

The air was filled once more with cheers.

"I'm Phineas," he went on, "and this is Ferb, and we're going to sing a song." He began to sing and strum his guitar.

The Ferbettes sang too. With each new lyric, they moved together.

Candace turned from her brother to the audience. The crowd was singing along with every word and doing all the moves the band

did. Honestly, it was almost as if they were in some sort of Ferbette trance or something!

Bouncing and singing, Phineas made his way over to his sister. Then he stopped and pointed to her. "Candace!"

Candace stood there in the spotlight as the whole mall waited for her to sing. She looked down at the lyrics sheet. Then she looked over at Phineas. Slowly, her eyes narrowed and she ground her teeth.

"Wait a minute!!!" she shouted. The sheet music went flying, and she balled her hands into tight fists. "*What* are you doing?"

"I'm cueing you," Phineas answered, still pointing and poised to go on.

"How did *you* get a hit single?" Candace hollered.

"Well, it wasn't easy," said Phineas with a matter-of-fact nod. "It took most of the morning and half a dozen phone calls, but if you're willing to put in the work—"

Candace felt as if she might explode—right then and there. Talk about not fair! Phineas and Ferb weren't even *musical*! And here they were, landing in the spotlight, just the same as always!

"That's it!" she fumed, throwing her arms into the air. Then she glared at Phineas and pointed. "I'm going to tell Mom!"

"Okay . . ." replied Phineas slowly. "Tell her . . . what?"

Candace thought for a moment. "Grr," she groaned, frustrated. For once, she didn't exactly know.

She turned and stormed across the stage. "I'm just gonna tell!!!" she huffed.

Phineas watched her go. Then he shrugged as the Ferbettes shuffled over to finish the song.

"Mom! Mom! Mom!" Candace ran across the mall into the boutique where her mom was shopping. "Mom, you've got to see this!"

Linda turned from the rack of clothes.

"Let me guess," she said, knowing that Candace was *always* trying to show her some crazy thing having to do with Phineas and Ferb. "Is it unbeliev—"

But Candace didn't let her finish. Instead,

she bulldozed her out of the store and across the mall, shouting, "Come on! Come on! Come on!"

She stopped, at last, just in front of the stage.

"See?" Candace said breathlessly. She pointed up at two shadows falling from behind a curtain that was about to be raised. "There they are, onstage!"

Just then, the announcer's voice came over the PA. "Ladies and gentlemen, once again . . . Marty the Rabbit Boy and His Musical Blender!"

The curtain went up . . .

. . . And there stood a rabbit boy, and his blender—which was oddly Ferb-shaped.

"Come on," Linda said, taking Candace by the arm. "We're going to get you an eye exam."

Meanwhile, across town Perry the Platypus was just arriving at the new, high-rise offices of Doofenshmirtz Evil, Incorporated.

"Everything is ready!" gloated the villain, rubbing his hands together as he reviewed the blueprints for his latest dastardly plan.

Ding-dong. The bell on the door of Dr. Doofenshmirtz's office suite rang.

"Oh, what is it now?" he groaned.

He opened the door to find Perry, still wearing his undercover funny-nose-and-glasses disguise.

"Oh! Are you my new temp?" asked Dr. Doofenshmirtz, not recognizing Perry. "Well, let me get you up to speed." He ushered in the disguised secret agent and led him past his papers and a half-eaten tuna sandwich to an impressive, state-of-the-art control room, complete with a giant blinking video map of the world.

"I know it's a bit of a mess," he went on. "I'm just putting the finishing touches on my latest maniacal plan. You'll see, in a few minutes," he explained, his voice growing more demented and evil-sounding with each word. "I will unleash an unprecedented reign of terror upon the entire—" he held a magnifying glass up to the middle of his map and enlarged a small area on the eastern coast of the United States "—tristate area. And Perry the Platypus," he added with glee, "will never be the wiser!"

Perry stared up at him and whipped off his disguise dramatically.

"Ah!" Dr. Doofenshmirtz gasped. "Perry the Platypus! You're a *temp*?" he asked, surprised. "Are times that hard?"

But he soon realized that Perry was doing the same job he'd always done—attempting to foil the doctor's plans.

"Sorry, Perry the Platypus," he said, smirking, "but you are too late."

He reached for a giant lever and pulled it. The building around them began to shake, and, within seconds, what had seemed like a regular office high-rise transformed into a thirty-story robot with long, pincer arms and feet the size of locomotives. Perry was now

33

trapped inside a giant robot with Dr. D.

"Ha-ha-ha-ha!" laughed Dr. Doofenshmirtz as his robot rose up from the ground and began to stomp across the city.

"When it comes to havoc," the villain crowed, "nobody wreaks it like me!"

But Perry wasn't about to let Dr. Doofenshmirtz destroy the entire city of Danville—or the tristate area! While Dr. D.'s back was turned, he yanked a panel out of the wall and touched two wires together. The robot turned and marched in the opposite direction.

"Whoa! Wait, wait!" the villain cried when he saw what Perry was doing. "You're not supposed to touch that! Hey! No fair! Very clever, Perry the Platypus. I was trying to ignore you, but you've forced my hand." He reached for a button over his shoulder and pressed it—hard. Instantly, mechanical arms sprang out of the wall and clamped around Perry.

"And now . . ." said Dr. Doofenshmirtz, as he finished reprogramming the robot to continue its destruction, "I shall relax with a nice, tasty deli platter." He sat down and began to fill a plate with salami, olives, and cheese from a large selection in the center of the table. The robot stomped along, crushing buildings,

parks, cars, and anything else in its path, while Dr. D. looked with delight at the food in front of him. It was well known that few things went with mayhem and destruction quite like a fine deli platter.

"Oh-ho-ho! Where are my manners?" He looked over at his prisoner, who was pinned to the wall. With all the charm of a gracious host, he fixed a plate for Perry.

"Here you go, Perry the Platypus," he said, setting it down on a nearby table. "Care for some pepper?" He pulled out a pepper mill. "Just say when. . . ."

He leaned over Perry's plate and began to grind away. Perry didn't say when, so Dr. D. kept on grinding.

"Any time . . ." The pile of pepper grew higher and higher.

Perry surely would have smiled . . . if only platypuses could.

Back at the mall, Candace was fuming. First she'd had to deal with Phineas and the Ferb-Tones, and now her mother had outfitted her in a brand-new pair of hideous, black-rimmed glasses.

"Argh. I told Mom I don't need glasses!" she muttered as she stomped out of the mall. "What the . . ."

Candace blinked, then blinked again. She yanked off her glasses and stared straight ahead.

No way! she thought. But there it was, as plain as day: a bus with Phineas and Ferb's faces and P.F.T. all over it!

Well, at least, Candace thought, her mom would believe her now.

Or would she? The bus was pulling away!

"No! No! Wait!" Candace begged, calling after the bus.

But hang on!

Was that a picture of Phineas and Ferb plastered across the side of an office building? Candace grinned and headed back into the mall. "Oh, *Mo-om!*" she called.

She ran through the mall until she finally found her mother in a department store.

"Mom!" cried Candace, grabbing Linda by the arm. "Come here, you've got to see this!"

"But Candace," said Linda, who was still trying on a jacket, "I haven't paid for this yet!"

Candace didn't care. She dragged her mom right out of the store, jacket and all.

Woo-woo-woo! went the alarm as Candace and her mom passed through the detector at the door.

"Hey!" yelled a security guard as he started chasing them through the mall.

"See?" cried Candace as she led her mom outside. She watched her mom's face as she pointed behind her to the wall where she'd seen the huge sign for P.F.T.

Linda looked where Candace was pointing and said nothing. Curious, Candace turned around.

"*Aaagh!*" she screamed. The building wasn't there!

That particular building had resided directly in the path of Dr. Doofenshmirtz's building-robot and had been demolished only seconds

 39

before Candace arrived with her mother.

Candace stood frozen, trying to figure out where the building had gone while the mall guard walked up and nodded sternly at Linda. "Uh, ma'am?" he said. "You're going to have to come back and pay for that."

"Yes, of course, officer," she replied, blushing.

As Linda followed the guard back inside, he turned to look at her more closely. "Hey, weren't you Lindana?" he suddenly said.

Linda smiled shyly. "Yes, I was," she said with a chuckle. "I can't believe you recognized me."

"Well, I was a *huge* fan," he told her. "I loved that hit single you had in the '80s—'I'm Lindana and I Want to Have Fun.' "

Linda smiled more brightly. Somebody actually remembered her!

"You still have to pay for the jacket," he said.

Linda nodded. "I know," she said with a sigh.

So many things were happening at once. Dr. Doofenshmirtz's pepper pile was growing higher and higher. The giant robot was marching on. Candace's blood was boiling, and her mother was paying for her new jacket. And in yet another part of the city, the biggest record company in the world was offering Phineas and Ferb the deal of a lifetime.

Chapter 5

"Boys," said Ben Baxter, the president of Huge "O" Records, "let me start by saying, we love your act, and we want to be in the Phineas and the Ferb-Tones business." He gestured to the other executives gathered around the conference table. "Uh, by the way," he added skeptically, "aren't you a little *young* to be pop stars?"

Phineas and Ferb exchanged a look on their

side of the table, then turned back to Ben. "No," Phineas replied.

"Well, okay, then!" Ben flashed a wide smile and quickly whipped out a large stack of papers. "We're prepared to offer you a *very* lucrative contract . . . if you'll just sign exclusively with us for your follow-up single."

"Follow-up single?" Phineas stood up, outraged, and leaned across the table. "Who do you think we are? Some two-bit hacks who'll keep writing new songs just because you'll pay us obscene amounts of cash?" He reached out and grabbed Ben Baxter's contract and bitterly tore it into pieces. "Phineas and the Ferb-Tones are strictly a one-hit wonder!" he declared. "Good day to you, sir!"

And together with Ferb, Isabella, and the rest of the one-hit-wonder Ferb-Tones, Phineas marched out of the conference room without looking back.

Satisfied, Phineas pulled out his checklist as they waited for the elevator. "Diva tantrum . . . check!" he said, marking off the second item on his list.

The elevator doors opened and the group stepped in. As the doors slid shut again and they began to descend to the ground floor, Phineas listened for a moment to the catchy, mellow tune drifting down from overhead. It was their song!

"Elevator music . . . check!" This was easier than he'd thought it would be!

Back inside the conference room, Ben Baxter merely shrugged.

hit record ✓
diva tantrum ✓
elevator music ✓
reunion tour ☐

"Ah, who needs 'em?" he said. He held up a tape and his eyes flashed. "We've still got this videotape of their performance. We can do live CDs, DVDs, podcasts! Heck," he went on, "we can digitally re-create their images to make our own sitcom—*The Phineas and Ferb Show*! We can squeeze twenty years of entertainment out of this one videotape!"

He was so excited about the gold mine in his hand that he didn't even realize what was happening outside the window behind him.

Across the room, another executive jumped up and pointed out the window. "Ah!" he cried. "That giant robot is coming right at us!"

Ben Baxter turned around . . . and could not believe his eyes.

Sure enough, as it continued on its path of destruction, Dr. Doofenshmirtz's giant robot was just about to crush the Huge "O" Records headquarters.

Inside the robot, however, Dr. Doofenshmirtz was still earnestly grinding away at the pepper mill.

"Wow, you sure like a lot of pepper," he told Perry, as the mountain of spice grew. "I'm more of a paprika man myself."

Perry eyed the pile, then closed his eyes. With the cool resolution of a seasoned spy, he blew hard at the pile of pepper.

A cloud of spicy black dust erupted and filled the air.

"*Kwahh-kuhh-kegh-kah!*" The villain coughed. But he was not to be deterred so easily. "It will take more than condiments to foil my brilliant plan!" he spat as he waved the cloud away. His eyes grew wide as a deep, bellowing sound began to echo all around them. The floor, walls, and ceiling began to tremble and quake.

"*Ah . . . ah . . . ah . . . CHOOOOO!*"

The robot was sneezing! As it did, it shot Dr. D. and Perry out of its robot mouth. They went tumbling into the air and straight through the window of

47

the conference room at Huge "O" Records.

They hurtled past the stunned record executives. "The tape!" hollered Ben Baxter as Perry flew by and snatched it out of his hands.

"Aaagh!" cried Dr. Doofenshmirtz as he and Perry crashed through the opposite wall and fell, head over heels, toward the ground thirty stories below.

Cool, calm, and collected as always, Perry grabbed hold of the videotape and pulled it smoothly out of its case. Then he tossed it around a flagpole like a rope as he shot past. He used the tape to swing himself safely around and onto the pole—while Dr. Doofenshmirtz kept falling.

"*Aaagh!*" the villain hollered. Bracing himself for the worst, he landed with a surprising *boing!* He'd fallen onto a mattress truck!

"Phew!" sighed Dr. Doofenshmirtz. "What an unbelievable stroke of luck!"

But Dr. D.'s luck was not quite as good as

48

he thought. He had landed on an Amazing Folding Mattress Company mattress. Before he knew what was happening, it folded in half like a taco—with him inside.

"Oh!" he groaned. Then he sighed. "I'm okay. Still better than—"

BOOM!

The foot of his broken robot crashed down on top of him.

"Curse you, Perry the Platypus!" Dr. Doofenshmirtz mumbled from under the robot's two-ton boot. Thanks to Perry, he'd been foiled again!

Phineas and the *ex-Ferb-Tones* were just getting off the elevator, completely unaware of the chaos and destruction the robot was wreaking outside.

They walked out the Huge "O" record

company doors to find Perry, back on all fours, strolling by.

"Oh, there you are, Perry," said Phineas—clueless, as always, about his pet platypus's secret life. "Come on, guys!" he called, leading the group to the bus stop. "We still have one thing left to do."

Chapter 6

Back at the mall, the television announcer was just taking the stage.

"And the winner of today's *Super American Pop Teen Idol Star* is . . ." He stepped aside as the curtain behind him rose. "Marty the Rabbit Boy and His Musical Blender!"

The long-eared musician patted his blender and took a bow.

"Oh, give him a hand!" the announcer went on. "He's going to Hollywood!"

From a bench not too far away, Candace looked on glumly.

"Hey, Candace," said a gentle voice from behind her.

It was Jeremy.

He sat down beside her—but even that didn't cheer Candace up.

"What's wrong?" he asked.

Candace sighed and pointed over to the bug-eyed rabbit boy. "I'm better than that guy!" she told Jeremy. "Oh!" She shook her head. "I should've taken blender lessons," she groaned.

"So why did you run off earlier?" Jeremy asked her, confused.

Candace clenched her fists and narrowed her eyes. "My brothers!" she said hotly. "They always ruin everything!"

Jeremy shrugged. "Well . . . you like to sing, right?" he said.

Candace looked over at him. "Yeah," she answered.

"Then you shouldn't let your brothers' fun ruin *your* good time. You know," Jeremy went on, "if you get the chance to sing, you ought to sing." He put his hand on Candace's shoulder. "I gotta go," he told her. "I'll see you later."

Candace smiled as he walked away. She stared happily after him until she heard someone else call out her name.

"Hey, Candace!" It was Phineas on the microphone, back up on stage. He had his guitar around his neck, and Ferb was beside him, ready with his keyboard and drums.

The band was back together again! And a

crowd was rapidly gathering around them.

"You're still the hundredth contestant!" Phineas went on. "Want to come up and help us out?"

Candace stood and squared her shoulders, thinking of Jeremy's words as she did. She took a deep breath—Phineas wouldn't have to ask her again. In an instant, she'd joined him onstage.

Each time it was Candace's turn to sing, she gave it her all. She really *did* love being on the stage.

"That was great!" Candace exclaimed as the song ended. The audience whistled and cheered so loudly she felt like an  honest-to-goodness pop star. It was almost too good to be true!

She held her hands up and let the audience's adoration sink in.

"Thanks, you've been great!" called out Phineas, as he stepped up to the mic  and waved. "This is the last time we'll ever sing that song! We're retiring. Good night!"

Candace froze, her arms still up, as she watched him and the rest of the Ferb-Tones turn and casually walk away.

CLICK. THWONK.

The lights went off, and an announcement

came over the PA: "The mall is now closed and will reopen at nine a.m. tomorrow. Thank you for shopping with us."

Retiring? She couldn't believe it!

Candace had come so close to being a pop star! But, thanks to her brothers, she'd been foiled again!

Part Two

Chapter 1

It was another sunny summer morning. Phineas and Ferb were outside, and Candace was in her room practicing lines for her role in the fall drama-club production. Sure, it was still summer, but you couldn't be too prepared. Candace had gone over the lines again and again . . . and again.

"*To think, to dream. Whether 'tis nobler to love, I know not.*"

She sighed and clutched her well-worn script to her chest in a tight hug.

"Ah, *The Princess Sensibilities*, my very favorite play . . ."

Grrrr. Growwwl. GAAAHHHH!

She frowned at the truly dreadful sounds coming from the backyard. She'd been hearing them all morning long. How was an actress to concentrate?

"What is going *on* out there?" she huffed. Whatever it was, she was going to stop it.

Rrroarrr! Grrrrr! RRAAAHHHH!

BAM! CRASH! BOOM!

Outside, Phineas and Ferb had built a miniature city, and Ferb was now happily destroying it with a fierce green monster marionette. Phineas was recording the whole thing with his video camera.

Hands on her hips, Candace stomped down squarely on the monster puppet (and a few cardboard houses, too) and glared at the puppet strings dangling limply from Ferb's hand. Then she turned her stern gaze on her brothers.

"Would you keep it down out here?" Candace snapped. "You guys ruin everything! I am trying to practice the art of acting! And I will not be disturbed by your little movies!"

"Not so little anymore," Phineas said brightly. He lowered his video camera and grinned. "Last week our Web site got a

hundred and seventy-six million hits!"

A hundred and seventy-six *million*? Before Candace could process the number, up walked her mother with her arms full of grocery bags.

"Sorry I'm late," she told the kids. "They're filming down the street."

Candace's eyes widened. "*Filming*? What? What are they filming?" she asked.

"A movie version of the play *The Princess Sensibilities*," said her mom casually, as she continued on into the house.

"*Oh!*" Candace gasped. "I would be perfect for that part!" She held up the script. "I've been practicing it for my drama club all summer," she said excitedly. "I'm going to get *discovered!*" She dashed off and tossed her script into the air.

"That's *serendipitous*," said Phineas, as he and Ferb watched her go. He glanced around the yard. "Hey, where's Perry?" Their pet platypus had been out in the yard with them all morning but was now nowhere to be seen.

Of course, they didn't know that Perry wasn't really the mild-mannered, slow-moving, dim-witted pet he seemed to be. He was a supersecret agent, known to his superiors as Agent P. At that very moment, Perry was up on two feet, dressed in his signature hat, and sitting in his secret cave beneath Phineas and Ferb's house, receiving orders via satellite from Major Monogram.

"There you are, Agent P!" said Major Monogram as Perry settled into the chair before the huge monitor displaying his image. "There's something very strange going on with Dr. Doofenshmirtz."

A picture of Perry's nemesis in a lab coat, grinning goofily while relaxing on a sunny, tropical-looking beach, popped up on the video screen.

"He's been very quiet lately," Major Monogram went on gravely. "A little *too* quiet!"

He brought up a graph on the screen that charted a steep decline in the villain's recent activity.

"I want you to find out what's *not* going on," he explained to Perry, "and, uh . . ." —he paused, realizing how unusual his request might seem— ". . . put a . . . stop . . . to it . . ."

He shifted his mustache. "I s'pose."

No mission was too illogical for Agent P. In an instant, he'd spun his seat around and pulled a lever on the side, sending the chair shooting up like a rocket toward the street.

"Good luck, Agent P!" Major Monogram called after him.

Perry's rocket seat blasted through the asphalt (missing the manhole he'd been aiming for by a few inches, unfortunately) and shot into the sky above the street. Once in the air, Perry coolly pushed another

65

lever, and a whirring helicopter propeller popped up above his chair.

Off he flew to defend justice by putting a stop to Doofenshmirtz's activities . . . or *non*-activities . . . or whatever exactly it was he had to do.

Chapter 2

As Agent P zoomed above the city, Candace quickly made her way down the street toward the movie set.

"There it is!" she gasped as she arrived, her eyes zeroing in on the producer's silver trailer.

She ran up to the door. It was open, so she peered in.

"Um . . . excuse me? Ahem . . . Mr. Producer, sir?" she said.

A grumpy-looking man with a goatee looked over his shoulder as he spoke into his cell phone. "I can't talk to you right now. My lead actress just quit!"

Candace stepped brightly into the trailer. "Well, sir," she said, "this is your lucky day!"

She cleared her throat and adjusted her expression into an appropriately princesslike one.

"To think!" Candace said, putting her hand to her head.

"To *dream!*" She clutched her chest.

"Whether 'tis nobler to love . . ." She fell to her knees dramatically. "I know not." She dropped her chin to her chest and bowed deeply.

The producer scratched his chin and

lowered his phone slowly. "Hmm . . . that's not bad . . . and you know your lines. Hmm . . ." He thought for a moment.

"I'll do it for free!" Candace blurted out.

"You're hired!" he said.

"Really?"

"You bet," the producer told her. He picked up his phone again and quickly began to punch in numbers. "With the money I save," he went on to himself, "I'll be able to hire the hottest new directors in town!" He grinned as his call went through. "Hello."

Candace, of course, was ecstatic. She'd actually landed the lead in the film version of her all-time favorite play! And not only that, she would be working with the best directors in town! At last, she would get the respect and attention a true artist like herself so richly deserved.

A short time later, Candace was in hair and makeup getting ready for her first scene. She wanted to pinch herself to make sure she wasn't dreaming.

"Wow!" she exclaimed blissfully as people flitted around to get her ready for filming. "I could get used to this!"

The assistant grip appeared with a clipboard and an assortment of other people.

"Miss Candace, here's your contract . . . and your bagel. This is Antoine, your dialogue coach; Mickey, your swimming stand-in; and your personal trainers, Olga and Chicago Jones." He held up a little box with two brawny crickets in it.

The smaller one chirped in a high voice, "Drop and give me twenty!"

How . . . exclusive, thought Candace.

It was time to head to the set. When she got there, the producer was waiting.

"Candace, *baby*, let me introduce you to the directors of this film." He motioned to a camera crane looming overhead and grinned as it lowered the two filmmakers toward them.

"Hi, Candace," said one director. His voice sounded familiar. . . .

Slowly, the two directors came into view.

"Phineas and Ferb?!" Candace cried. "What are you doing here?"

"We're directing the movie," said Phineas. "Our new agent arranged the whole thing." He pointed over his shoulder to his faithful friend Isabella, who was busy on her cell phone.

"Look," Candace could hear her saying,

"my client gets three percent of the gross and a piece of the back end or he walks. Yeah. That's right." She frowned. "You mess with the bull, you get the horns, buddy. Hello?" She hung up and took another call. "Syd, *baby*," she said, smiling, "you got that third act of mine yet?"

"Wait, wait!" wailed Candace. This simply couldn't be! Desperately, she grabbed the producer by the shoulders. "Don't you think they're a little *young* to be big-budget movie directors?" she asked him.

"With a hundred and seventy-six million hits," he told her, "they could be in diapers, for all I care." And with a wink to his new directors, he happily walked away.

Phineas nodded to Ferb. It was time for the moviemaking to begin!

Chapter 3

Later that day, after a trip to wardrobe, Candace found herself in a long blue satin princess gown, high-heeled silver slippers . . . and a huge, green, toothy monster head. In fact, she looked a lot like the puppet Ferb had been playing with in their backyard that morning—only a lot bigger and a little more dressed up.

"Phineas," she said, "I don't remember any monsters in *The Princess Sensibilities*."

"We just finished the rewrites this morning," he explained.

He held up the script, and she looked at the cover—the title had been crossed out and changed completely.

"*The Curse of the Princess Monster*?" Candace hollered. "That is not what I signed up for! Besides, I can't wear *this*!" she went on, yanking off the monster head. "No one will see my face!"

"Yes," said the producer, walking up behind her, "but in the end the curse is lifted, and in your big dramatic scene, you will look stunning! This film could make you . . . a *star*!"

"Really?" Candace reconsidered. She could almost see the limousines, long red carpets, and flashing lights of paparazzi in her future. She could almost feel the wet cement as she left her handprints in the Hollywood Walk of

Fame. She could see her name in lights and on the covers of all the magazines.

"A . . . a . . . *star*?" She sighed.

That was all he had to say.

"Hey, ugly monster," came a voice from outside the wardrobe trailer. "You're needed on the set!"

"I'm coming!" she sang.

And after a few tries, Candace got her fat, scaly head through the doorway. She was ready to begin her movie-star career!

On the other side of town, Perry—aka Agent P—had arrived at the *new* official headquarters of Doofenshmirtz Evil, Incorporated. Boldly, he crashed through the door, laser gun in hand, ready to foil whatever dastardly plot the evil genius was set to hatch.

"Perry the Platypus!" cried Dr. Doofenshmirtz. "Why do you keep breaking down my doors?" He got up from the easy chair where he'd been sitting quietly reading. "Why don't you knock first? It's not even locked!"

He looked around at the door and angrily surveyed the damage. "This time . . . you'll *pay!*" he sneered bitterly.

Perry froze. Then he shrugged and reached for his wallet.

"That's right," Dr. D. demanded. "Fork it over."

Dr. Doofenshmirtz took the bills Perry held out and counted them carefully. "*What*? Are you kidding me?" he asked, holding up Perry's cash. He pointed at the splinters of door scattered all over the floor. "That's not just drywall, you know. It's solid oak!"

Reluctantly, Perry dug out a few more bills, and the villain quickly grabbed them. "That's more like it. You can't just go busting into people's houses for no reason, you know," he scolded. "Besides," he added, "I've given up evil to pursue the art of cheesemaking!"

Perry looked at the book Dr. D. had been reading before he was interrupted: *The Art of Cheese*.

Grinning, Dr. Doofenshmirtz directed Perry's attention to the other side of his office, where

78

a pedestal displayed a giant wheel of extremely odorous cheese. "Do you like stinky Limburger?" he asked Perry. "It's a Doofenshmirtz family recipe!" His eyes were wide with craving and pride.

"It's not ready yet," he explained. "It still has to age for fifty-eight and a half years." He looked at his watch. "But—who's got that kind of time? Which is why," he went on, a shifty gleam in his eyes, "I created the Age-Accelerator . . . inator!"

With that, he pulled open a curtain to reveal his newest, most ingenious machine.

Chapter 4

Back at the movie set, the filming of *The Curse of the Princess Monster* was well under way.

"Okay, Candace," Phineas called from his director's chair, "this is a very important scene. It is nothing less than the emotional backbone of the whole film. Oh . . . and the villagers are coming at you with everything they've got."

Ferb clapped the film board, and the

camera began to roll.

Candace peered through her monster head at the tiny city set around her. It

looked a lot like the city she'd stomped through that morning in her own backyard.

"Uh, what do you mean, the villagers—" she began to ask.

"Action!" Phineas cried, and a battery of cardboard missiles came shooting at her from off-set.

Candace tried in vain to swat the weapons away.

Next, Phineas shouted, "The air force!" At that, Ferb began firing toy plane after toy plane through the air at her.

"Ugh! Oh! Oh! Hey! *Wait!*" Candace hollered. This was no "emotional" scene. She waved for her brothers to stop the tape, but it was no use.

"The space armada from the planet Plumbing Supplies!" Phineas ordered. Down from the rafters fell a claw-footed bathtub, a bunch of lead pipes, some sinks, and a toilet bowl.

"Oof!" Candace grunted as the barrage knocked her to the floor. "Ohhh . . ." That hurt.

"Beautiful!" declared Phineas. "That's a print!"

Candace tried to stay calm. She was in pain and hated the scene, but at least it was over.

Phineas started to move on to the next scene when one of the Fireside Girl crew members whispered something in his ear.

"Oh." He winced. "That's a little embarrassing." Phineas chuckled as he took the lens cap off the camera. They'd have to film the whole thing all over again!

He picked up his megaphone. "Okay,

people," he called out as Candace fumed. "Nice rehearsal. Let's take it from the top!"

The next scene had to be easier. Candace was sure of it.

"Wow," she said as Phineas replaced her monster head with a fancy new headpiece. "Is this banana hat for some cool tropical dance number?"

"We're trying to come up with some exciting camera angles for the big chase scene," Phineas explained. Then he pointed offstage to a ravenous-looking primate wearing its own fancy hat. "So we strapped a camera on this starving monkey."

Candace stared at the hungry animal and glanced at the bananas on her head. Then she ran, screaming, as the monkey chased her off the set.

"Get away! Get away! Get away!" she screeched as she raced away from the beast. After a few minutes, Phineas called off the monkey. Candace stopped and tried to catch her breath.

When the monkey was finally subdued, Phineas chuckled apologetically. "That monkey-cam didn't work out," he said. "We're going to try it with Ferb this time." He nodded to Ferb, who was wearing the camera on his head.

"Now," he told Candace as he placed a foot-long ham-and-cheese sandwich in her hands, "take this sandwich and remember, Ferb hasn't eaten lunch yet."

Candace's face froze in fear.

"Hold on tight," Phineas urged.

Ferb began to charge, and Candace ran for her life.

* * *

A little later, Candace was almost glad when she was told to put the monster head back on . . . but not for very long.

"Okay, in this scene the monster—that's you," Phineas said, pointing to Candace, "gets attacked by eight hundred cubic feet of rats, spiders, and snakes!"

Candace looked with disbelief at the three huge crates of vermin poised precariously above her.

"There is no way I'm doing that!" she declared, whipping off her monster head.

"Relax," said Phineas. He held up one of the snakes and jiggled it in his hand. "They're made out of rubber."

"Aahh." Candace sighed. Thank goodness, she thought. With Phineas, you never knew!

She put her monster head back on and took her mark in the middle of the miniature city.

Suddenly, she screamed as tons of very *real* rats and spiders suddenly engulfed her.

"Well, the *snakes* are rubber, anyway," Phineas said with a snicker.

It was time for the big glamour scene. The monster head was gone, and Candace's hair and makeup were done perfectly. All she had to do was lie in a real bed, like a real princess, and say the lines she'd always loved.

But Candace should probably have known better than to expect things to go the way she'd hoped.

"Okay, Candace, this is your beauty shot," Phineas reminded her, and she smiled. "The curse has been lifted and you're no longer a monster. Now, this scene is all about what the heart wants, but the mind can't have." He clapped the film board and nodded. "Take one."

"To *dream*," began Candace, throwing her hands up dramatically into the air. "To be *free* of the curse!"

"Beautiful!" Phineas called. "Keep going! Cue the magical girlie dust!" he shouted into his megaphone.

Above the set, Ferb tipped over a box full of glitter. The sparkles began to fall down onto Candace's head. At first, they drifted down gently.

"Whether 'tis nobler to be loved," said Candace, enjoying the sparkly effect. Then, suddenly, the whole box came crashing down on her head. "Aaah-*choo*!" She sneezed.

"Cue wind machine!" Phineas cried.

Ferb lifted a giant lever, and a jet turbine engine was instantly turned on. It swept away every speck of dust—and Candace, practically, too.

"To be . . . cursed . . . by love . . ." she gasped, clinging to the headboard of her bed with all her might to keep from being blown away. "Phineas!" she screamed finally, "make it *stop*!"

"Cut the wind machine!" he hollered.

Ferb lowered the lever and the gale-force winds stopped. Candace fell to the mattress with an "Oof!" But the scene wasn't over.

"Okay . . ." Phineas went on, as the camera kept rolling, ". . . drop the flower petals!"

"Whether 'tis nobler—" Candace muttered weakly. But before she could finish her lines, a load of plumbing supplies came crashing down from above.

Phineas looked up at Ferb. A full box

labeled FLOWER PETALS sat on the rafter next to him. "Wrong prop!" Phineas observed. "What the heck? Let's keep it! Okay, people. That's a wrap!"

The filming of *The Curse of the Princess Monster* was officially finished.

Chapter 5

Later that day in the editing room, Phineas and Ferb were busy turning all the scenes they'd shot into a cinematic masterpiece. The recording was playing on a large computer, and Ferb was meticulously cutting and pasting scenes into order. Candace sat miserably between them, gnawing at her fingers.

She watched scene after scene on the

computer. Just as Candace had feared, they were not pretty.

"Here's your big dramatic scene, Candace," Phineas said eagerly. She cringed as the bedroom came into view.

"To think . . . to—to stink . . . to . . . to—"

Candace winced as she watched herself lying there, gasping and panting, battered and banged and totally bruised.

"Oh," she moaned, pounding her head against the table. Tears poured out of her eyes like they were fountains. "This is horrible!" she wailed. "I can't let anybody see this!"

"That's what is called a *rough cut*," Phineas said cheerily. "Ferb's going to fix it in editing. Tighten up the dialogue," he explained as Ferb plugged away on the computer. "Do a little voice modulation. Play with the filters."

Candace could see *some* of what he was talking about on the monitor before them. The computer program seemed to change everything around. Mostly, though, she kept her eyes covered with her hands.

"And now, take a look," said Phineas finally.

Candace slowly and reluctantly slid open her fingers and peeked out at the screen.

"To think . . . to dream . . . to be free of the curse."

"*Ahhh!*" Candace gasped. There she was on the screen, looking positively awesome and gorgeous, speaking her lines perfectly— with real background music and everything!

"I . . . I . . . I look beautiful!" she squealed, clasping her hands together in glee.

"That's what they call *movie magic*," said Phineas.

"You two are the best brothers a great actress could ever have!" cried Candace. Then she threw her arms around them . . . something she'd never done before. She couldn't wait for the movie to premiere.

Academy Awards, look out! thought Candace. Here I come!

Chapter 6

Candace didn't have to wait long for the premiere. The producer set up a sneak preview before the day was through.

"We packed this theater with teenagers," he explained to Candace, Phineas, and Ferb, as they stood outside the movie house. "They're our target audience. If they like it, we're in business. If they don't . . ." He drew his finger sharply across his throat to indicate

that the whole project
would be dead.

Inside, the young audi-
ence quieted down as the
lights dimmed and the title
sequence began.

"The Curse of the Princess Monster!" said a
low, sinister voice.

Instantly, the whole place erupted in
cheers.

"Looks like we've got a hit movie!" declared
the producer.

Phineas and Ferb high-fived each other,
and Candace jumped for joy.

Whoopee! she thought. At last, her dreams
of movie stardom were really coming true!

A couple of blocks away, Dr. Doofenshmirtz
was showing Perry his very latest invention.

"Now, Perry the Platypus," he said as
they stood on a balcony high above the

unsuspecting city below, "watch carefully as I demonstrate the Age-Accelerator . . . inator!"

The device was strapped to his back and, as he jumped into the air, a laser shot out from the top and blasted a glowing green beam

through the sky. Dr. Doofenshmirtz aimed it at a park where children were playing, and the beam landed on a toddler who was happily riding a seesaw with another child.

Perry watched as the cute little toddler grew into a big, hairy adult. He got so heavy so

quickly that he sent the kid sitting on the other side of the seesaw flying through the air.

"Hooray, it works!" crowed Dr. Doofenshmirtz. "And now, to make some perfectly aged cheese!"

Still wearing his age-accelerating machine, Dr. D. strode back into his office and up to his big wheel of cheese. He took aim—and fired.

The cheese ripened before their eyes. "Ah, perfect!" he exclaimed, delighted, cutting off the laser. "You can actually see the pungent aroma!" He cut off a large, fragrant hunk and handed it to Perry. "Here you go, Perry the Platypus. But I'm warning you." He wagged his finger. "Once you start, you won't be able to stop."

Perry eyed the cheese skeptically. He didn't approve of the villain's methods . . . but his cheese did look good.

97

"I'll go get some crackers," Dr. Doofenshmirtz told him, heading toward the kitchen. He was back in a moment, carrying a tray.

"We're in luck," said Dr. Doofenshmirtz happily. "I still have some leftover melba—" But he stopped abruptly and froze in midstep. His hands started to shake, and he dropped the tray of crackers.

CRASH!

"Whoa! Oh, *no!*" he cried. Where moments before his perfect wheel of pungent cheese had gloriously rested, there was now only an empty pedestal. "The *cheese*! What happened to the stinky cheese? Perry the Platypus!" His eyes zeroed in on Perry—who looked more like a Frisbee than a platypus. "You ate all the cheese?" he wailed. "No! *No!*"

Perry tried to look innocent. But there was no hiding the

distinct wheel-shaped bulge in his belly. It had been fabulously irresistible cheese.

The villain looked up at the machine, which still hung heavily on his back. "I created this for peaceful, cheese-loving purposes," he moaned, "but now you force me to wield it in anger!"

He aimed the Age-Accelerator . . . inator at Perry and fired away.

But even filled with cheese, Perry was too quick for him.

"*Aargh!*" growled the villain as he kept wildly shooting. "Perry the Platypus, hold still! Hold still so I can blast you!"

As you may have guessed, Perry would do anything but hold still.

Back at the movie theater, the young audience was whooping and cheering like crazy.

"Wow, those kids *love* it!" the producer said with a laugh.

"Yay!" cried Candace. "Superstardom, here I come!"

But out of nowhere, a glowing green beam passed through the roof of the theater. A moment later, the sounds from inside became decidedly different.

"Boo! *Boo!*" The audience was livid!

"What's going on in there?" exclaimed Phineas.

Followed by Ferb and Candace, Phineas ran into the theater. He threw open the heavy doors and discovered a bunch of grumpy old people!

"It's too loud with all the rock and roll!" shouted one man.

"A waste of my time," grumbled another.

"Where are my teeth?" an old woman asked.

And out they shuffled in a surly, white-haired mass.

The producer stepped up with a handful of questionnaires collected from the audience. "Sorry, kids, they hated it," he said. "The movie's dead."

He turned and walked off, leaving Candace stunned and speechless.

"Well, at least we had fun!" said Phineas.

"*Fun?*" exclaimed Candace. "What about *me*? I was gonna be a *star!*" Had she really gone through all that torture for nothing? Nothing at all?

"Don't worry, Candace," Phineas told her. "We saved a copy of your best scenes. We're going to put it on our Web site right away!"

Well . . . thought Candace skeptically. Her brothers' site *did* get a lot of hits. Maybe she could still become famous.

They headed back home, completely unaware of the *real* drama unfolding thirty stories above their heads.

Igh in his office, the evil scientist Dr. Doofenshmirtz had Perry cornered at last. After all, a walking wheel of cheese can be only so nimble.

"Yah, ha, *ha*!" laughed Doofenshmirtz crazily. "I have you cornered!" His gizmo was set at DANGEROUSLY HIGH and poised to shoot.

"This time I'll hit you with everything I've

got!" Doofenshmirtz cried. "Say good-bye, Perry the Platypus!"

He pulled the trigger, and everything went green. But it was

only a second before the machine exploded, in a blast of noise and light! The room was filled with the screeching of metal being wrecked . . . and then everything fell eerily silent.

Dr. Doofenshmirtz peered through the smoke left by the explosion.

"Wait, wait, wait. That's not right," he muttered, as his ruined machine disintegrated. Then he looked down at Perry. "Oh, Perry the Platypus." He laughed. "Just . . . just look at yourself! You really let yourself go."

Sure enough, Perry appeared to have aged at least eighty years (and not gracefully, either). His fur was wrinkled. His beak was drooping. It was all he could do just to stand with the help of a cane.

Little did Dr. Doofenshmirtz know that *he* looked a *hundred* years older—and that Perry had a surprise up his wrinkled sleeve.

The platypus grabbed his chest and ripped off the sagging skin in a single, heroic movement. Underneath was good old *young* Perry, fit and ready to face crime head-on.

"Oh, so, you had on an Age-Accelerator-inator-proof suit, eh?" cackled Doofenshmirtz. "Well, I have a little surprise of my own!"

He grabbed his lab coat and tore it off (along with all his other clothes), just as Perry had, to reveal . . . an old man in droopy black socks and polka-dotted underwear! Dr. D.'s aging machine had been effective, indeed.

The old man sighed. "Well, it's already four thirty," Dr. Doofenshmirtz said, looking at his watch. He turned and scuffled off with a sigh. "I think I'm going to bed. *Hmph*." He coughed mildly. "Curse you, Perry the Platypus," he said unenthusiastically.

Back at home, Candace was getting her first look at Phineas and Ferb's webcast masterpiece.

"Oh, boy!" said Phineas, as the title came on the computer screen: *The Swamp Monster of Danville.*

"This is going to be great!"

Candace watched excitedly. But her face slowly fell as everyday white shoes came stomping into view on the screen. Where were the fancy costumes?

The shoes flattened a cardboard house . . . then promptly squashed an unsuspecting monster.

The shot shifted to a fierce, terrifying face— one that was *definitely* Candace's. No doubt whatsoever. Her eyes were wild, and her teeth were bared ferociously in rage.

"YOU . . . GUYS . . . RUIN . . . EVERY-THING!"

The words rumbled out of her mouth in slow motion.

As she watched in horror, Candace wanted to scream. Where was Candace the *princess*? Where were her dramatic *lines*? Where was the fabulous *beauty shot* Ferb had edited just that afternoon? This was nothing but the video they'd gotten of her storming in on them that morning!

She looked like a *monster*, Candace realized. And she sounded like one, too!

She, Candace, was the swamp monster of Danville!

If only she *were* a monster, then she could have stomped on them right then and there!

"Whoa, check it out!" exclaimed Phineas. He pointed to the number quickly rising at the bottom of the screen. "Five million hits already! I bet everyone we know saw it! Enjoy it while it lasts, Candace," he said, smiling up at his sister. "Fame is fleeting."

106

Candace winced. She could only hope so!

And then Ferb spoke up. "But the Internet is *forever*."

Candace moaned. Foiled *again*! She fainted and collapsed on the floor.

"Good night, Candace." Phineas grinned.

He wasn't sure why Candace wasn't thrilled. As far as he and Ferb were concerned, the film was evidence of another totally awesome summer day!

Don't miss the fun in the next
Phineas & Ferb book . . .

WILD SURPRISE

Adapted by Helena Mayer
Based on the series created by Dan Povenmire & Jeff "Swampy" Marsh

Phineas Flynn popped up in bed, his eyes wide open.

"Hey, Ferb!" Phineas tossed a pillow across the room, aiming for his brother, who was still fast asleep. Phineas didn't get it. How could Ferb sleep on a day like this?

After all, it wasn't just any day.

This was it, the big day. The day Phineas had been waiting for all summer long. "It's Candace's birthday!" he shouted, blasting

Ferb out of dreamland. "We gotta do better than last year."

Last year's birthday had started out okay.

Candace had loved her cake. It was chocolate chocolate chip (her favorite) and covered in pink and white frosting (her double favorite).

But Phineas had made a big mistake. It never occurred to him that Candace would want to *eat* the cake. Eating was seriously dullsville and Phineas had something much more exciting in mind. Something like a giant gorilla hiding inside the cake, waiting to jump out when Phineas yelled, "Happy birthday, Candace!"

It also never occurred to Phineas that Candace was afraid of gorillas.

Especially giant gorillas hiding inside of birthday cakes.

"Not our best work," Phineas admitted. Ferb didn't say anything, but Phineas could

tell he agreed. "This time, it's gotta be something huge!"

This year, Phineas was determined to give his sister a birthday present that wouldn't make her scream and run out of the room. And he knew just how to do it.